CAPTAINS OUTRAGEOUS

Adapted by
Don Ferguson

Illustrated by
Vaccaro Associates, Inc.

MALLARD
PRESS

Twin Books

The Jungle Aces Adventure Club was having a meeting. "This is Oscar Van Der Snoot," Kit said, introducing his friend to the other members of the club. "Oscar wants to be a Jungle Ace!"

"Have you had any adventures, Oscar?" the club
president asked.

"No," he answered. "My mother thinks adventures
aren't safe!"

Ernie just shook his head.

5

"Sorry, Oscar," he said. "The Jungle Aces Club is just for kids who have adventures!"

"That's okay," Oscar said sadly. "If it was my club, I wouldn't want me either!"

Suddenly Kit said, "Come on, Oscar! I have an idea!"
Oscar followed Kit out of the clubhouse. "Where are
we going?" he asked.
"You'll find out soon enough!" Kit answered.
Oscar's first real adventure had begun.

At that very moment, two of Don Karnage's evil air pirates—Mad Dog and Dump Truck—were spying on the boys. "The rich kid and Kit just came out of the clubhouse, Boss!" Mad Dog whispered into his walkie-talkie.

"Then follow them!" Karnage commanded.

Karnage was planning to kidnap Oscar and hold him for ransom. "Wait until he's alone, then grab him!" he instructed Mad Dog and Dump Truck.

Keeping out of sight, the pirates followed the two boys.

"Well, we're here!" Kit finally said.

"Where?" Oscar asked.

"Higher for Hire!" Kit replied. "Our base of operations!"

Baloo was snoozing under the *Sea Duck*'s wing.

"That's Baloo," Kit explained. "He's storing up energy for our next adventure!

"And this is Wildcat, our mechanical genius!" Kit said. Wildcat was holding a big wrench, trying to turn a valve on a red metal tank.

"Pleased to meet . . ." Oscar began, when suddenly the valve on the tank broke off!

Whoosh! The tank took off like a rocket! First it zoomed by the sleeping Baloo, knocking him out of his hammock. Then it turned and picked up speed. The two spying air pirates saw it coming, but there was no time to duck!

In a moment, Mad Dog and Dump Truck were airborne, hanging on to the rocketing tank for dear life. They lost their grip just as the tank went over the shore. *Splash!* Into the water they went.

Inside the Higher for Hire office, Oscar exclaimed,
"Wow, that was some secret weapon!" Wildcat started
to say it was just a tankful of gas, but Kit signalled
him to be quiet. Let Oscar think it was a secret weapon.
After all, this was going to be his first adventure.

But from the office's open window, Mad Dog and
Dump Truck were listening to every word. "So that's
what that thing was!" Dump Truck said.
"Let's see what else we can find out," said Mad Dog.
They edged closer to the window, hoping to hear more.

Rebecca came into the office, and Kit told her about Oscar and the Jungle Aces Club. "Couldn't Oscar fly with Baloo tomorrow, when he delivers the secret weapon?" Kit winked at Rebecca.

"Secret weapon . . . oh, yes—the secret weapon!"
Rebecca said. "Oscar can go with Baloo to deliver the
secret weapon if his mother gives him permission."

Outside the window, Mad Dog and Dump Truck
whispered into the walkie-talkie.

"Baloo and Oscar are delivering the secret weapon tomorrow morning, chief!" Mad Dog reported.

"Great!" Don Karnage's voice replied. "Now I can get Oscar and the secret weapon at the same time! You two get back here right now!" he ordered. "I've got a new plan."

Oscar went home to get his mother's permission. And Kit began to create a plan for an adventure.

"Tomorrow Wildcat and I will disguise ourselves as air
pirates," Kit told Baloo and Wildcat. "Then we'll pretend
to attack the *Sea Duck*."

"That'll really give Oscar an adventure," Baloo chortled.

Wildcat said, "I guess I'd better get busy rigging
up another 'secret weapon'!"

Early the next morning, a very long limousine brought Oscar and his mother to Higher for Hire. "Are you sure this will be quite safe?" Mrs. Van Der Snoot asked Rebecca. "Oscar is very delicate!"

"Absolutely safe," Rebecca assured her.

"Very well, Oscar dear. You may go," Mrs. Van Der Snoot said.

"Yippee!" said Oscar and Baloo together.

"Where's Kit and Wildcat?" Oscar asked.

"They had to . . . uh . . . run an errand," Baloo said.
"I guess that makes you my copilot, Oscar."

Inside the sea plane, Oscar saw Wildcat's propane tank. "The secret weapon!" he said excitedly.

"Shh! Not so loud," said Baloo, sitting down at the controls.

24

"Sorry," said Oscar, taking the seat beside him.

The *Sea Duck's* engines roared to life. The plane skimmed across the water, then lifted its nose into the sky.

Kit and Wildcat had taken off earlier in another plane. Now they were flying above the clouds, waiting for the *Sea Duck* to appear.

"Any minute now," Kit said, straightening his disguise.

Suddenly a dark shadow fell across their plane. Looking up, Kit saw the sinister shape of Don Karnage's *Iron Vulture*. In a second, the *Vulture's* bay doors opened and Kit and Wildcat's airplane was swept inside.

Back in the *Sea Duck*, Baloo chuckled, imagining what Oscar would do when he saw the two make-believe pirates. But seconds later it was the *Iron Vulture*, not Kit and Wildcat, he saw heading straight for them.

Trying to escape, Baloo steered the *Sea Duck* into
Skull Cave.

Don Karnage's voice crackled over the *Sea Duck's*
radio. "Surrender, Baloo! I have captured Kit and Wildcat."

"Okay, Karnage," Baloo answered. "You win."

As the *Sea Duck* left the cave, Baloo took two sacks of potatoes out of the cargo hold. He put parachutes on them and threw them overboard.

Don Karnage saw the sacks as they floated down to earth.

"Drat! They've bailed out!" he snarled.

Baloo and Oscar hid in the *Sea Duck*'s secret
compartment. "Why didn't we blast 'em with the secret
weapon?" Oscar asked.

"It's a phony," Baloo answered. "We told you it was a
secret weapon to make your adventure more exciting."

Just then, Don Karnage lifted the plane into the belly of the *Iron Vulture*. Then he and his pirates boarded the *Sea Duck* and found the 'secret weapon.'

"Let's get Kit and Wildcat to show us how to use this thing. We can fish the rich kid out of the water later," Karnage said.

31

Baloo crept out of the hiding place, carrying several
sticks of dynamite. "Karnage probably has Kit and
Wildcat locked up in the brig," he told Oscar. "I'll blast
the door down and get 'em. You wait for me right here."
At the brig door, Baloo discovered he had no matches.

Just then, the door flew open and Mad Dog grabbed Baloo and dragged him inside.

"So! You thought you had tricked me!" said Don Karnage. "Show me how to work the secret weapon!"

Now Kit, Wildcat, *and* Baloo were trapped in the brig with Don Karnage and his gang. Then—*boom!*—the door was blown off its hinges.

"You forgot your matches, Baloo. So I lit the dynamite myself!" Oscar announced proudly.

Karnage grabbed Oscar's shirt. "Perhaps my newest prisoner will tell me how to work the secret weapon," he said.

"Okay," Oscar replied.

Baloo, Kit, and Wildcat looked at each other. What was Oscar up to?

"I'll need a wrench," Oscar said, remembering what had happened when Wildcat tried to open the tank valve.

Don Karnage found a wrench and handed it over. Oscar tugged at the valve with all his might.

Whoosh! Once again, the tank blasted off like a rocket. It picked up Karnage and rocketed him around the room, knocking his air pirates over like a bowling ball.

"Let's get out of here!" shouted Baloo.

Baloo, Oscar, Kit, and Wildcat raced down the narrow corridors of the *Iron Vulture*, chased by the runaway tank. The helpless Don Karnage still clung to its back. The tank zoomed out of sight toward the cargo bay that held the *Sea Duck*. Then there was a loud explosion.

"Oh, no!" said Baloo. "Look at our plane!"
The tank had blown up, ripping a giant opening
in the floor of the hangar. The *Sea Duck* teetered on
the hole's edge.

"It's going to fall! Quick, get in!" Baloo shouted.
Baloo, Kit and Wildcat scrambled into the teetering
plane. But just as Oscar was about to join them, the
Sea Duck tipped away from him.

The plane continued to rock, then fell through the hole in the floor. Oscar slipped and followed the *Sea Duck* as it plunged through the sky toward the ocean.

While Baloo and Wildcat tried to get the *Sea Duck*'s engines started, Kit grabbed his air foil and jumped out the rear hatch of the sea plane. Above him, Kit saw Oscar falling.

As Kit reached out his hand and caught Oscar, the *Sea Duck*'s engines finally kicked in.

Both boys held onto the air foil, skimming along behind the sea plane like two water-skiers.

Back at Higher for Hire, Oscar's mother waited for the *Sea Duck*'s return. Suddenly the sea plane zoomed by overhead, with Kit and Oscar trailing behind on the air foil.

"Hi, Mom! Yah-hooo!" Oscar called out.

Mrs. Van Der Snoot fainted.

The next day the story of Oscar's adventure was in the news.

Oscar's mother read about it in the paper and fainted again.

Cape Suzette Gazette

25¢

JUNGLE ACES ADVENTURE CLUB FOILS KIDNAPPING ATTEMPT

Kidnappers Left Up in the Air

When the Jungle Aces held their next meeting, Oscar was officially made a member. Not only that, but he was elected by a unanimous vote to be honorary president.

"Not bad for a first adventure," said Kit, with a wink.